VANCOUVER PUBLIC LIBR

S0-AKS-196

Halloween

A Level Two Reader

By Cynthia Klingel and Robert B. Noyed

The **Child's World®**

Boo! It is time for Halloween.

Halloween is on October 31.

It started in other countries

a long time ago.

Halloween colors are orange and black. Pictures of witches, ghosts, and black cats are everywhere.

Children do many fun things for Halloween. At school, they decorate their classroom.

Many people carve pumpkins into jack-o'-lanterns. The jack-o'-lanterns sit on doorsteps or in windows.

Children choose or make costumes to wear. Some costumes are scary. Some are funny.

Many people like to have Halloween parties. They play Halloween games.

When it gets dark, children visit neighbors they know. They knock on doors and shout, "Trick or treat!"

Neighbors give the children treats. The children get many tasty treats to eat.

Boo! Halloween is a fun
night for children.

Index

To Find Out More

Books

Prelutsky, Jack. *It's Halloween.* New York: William Morrow, 1996.

Ross, Kathy. *Crafts for Halloween.* Brookfield, Conn.: Millbrook Press, 1994.

Stevens, Kathryn. *Halloween Jack-o'-Lanterns.* Chanhassen, Minn.: Child's World, 2000.

Web Sites

Celebrate! Holidays in the U.S.A.: Halloween
http://www.usemb.se/Holidays/celebrate/hallowee.html
For an article about Halloween from a U.S. embassy.

Tricks, Treats, Costumes, & Safety
http://www.redcross.org/tips/october/octtips.html
For information about Halloween safety from the American Red Cross.

Note to Parents and Educators

Welcome to Wonder Books®! These books provide text at three different levels for beginning readers to practice and strengthen their reading skills. Additionally, the use of nonfiction text provides readers the valuable opportunity to *read to learn*, not just to learn to read.

These leveled readers allow children to choose books at their level of reading confidence and performance. Nonfiction Level One books offer beginning readers simple language, word choice, and sentence structure as well as a word list. Nonfiction Level Two books feature slightly more difficult vocabulary, longer sentences, and longer total text. In the back of each Nonfiction Level Two book are an index and a list of books and Web sites for finding out more information. Nonfiction Level Three books continue to extend word choice and length of text. In the back of each Nonfiction Level Three book are a glossary, an index, and a list of books and Web sites for further research.

State and national standards in reading and language arts emphasize using nonfiction at all levels of reading development. Wonder Books® fill the historical void in nonfiction material for primary grade readers with the additional benefit of a leveled text.

About the Authors

Cynthia Klingel has worked as a high school English teacher and an elementary school teacher. She is currently the curriculum director for a Minnesota school district. Cynthia lives with her family in Mankato, Minnesota.

Robert B. Noyed started his career as a newspaper reporter. Since then, he has worked in school communications and public relations at the state and national level. Robert lives with his family in Brooklyn Center, Minnesota.

Published by The Child's World®, Inc.
PO Box 326
Chanhassen, MN 55317-0326
800-599-READ
www.childsworld.com

Special thanks to the first grade students of Middleton School, their parents,
and teacher (Julie Marcus) for their help and cooperation in preparing this book.

Photo Credits
© David Young-Wolff/PhotoEdit: 6, 17, 18
© 2003 David Young-Wolff/Stone: 13
© Martin R. Jones/Unicorn Stock Photos: 14
© North Wind Pictures: 5
© 1999 Patti McConville/Dembinsky Photo Assoc. Inc.: 21
© Richard Hutchings/PhotoEdit: cover
© Romie Flanagan: 9, 10
© Tom McCarthy/Photri, Inc.: 2

Project Coordination: Editorial Directions, Inc.
Photo Research: Alice K. Flanagan

Copyright © 2003 by The Child's World®, Inc.
All rights reserved. No part of this book may be
reproduced or utilized in any form or by any means
without written permission from the publisher.
Printed in the United States of America.

Library of Congress Cataloging-in-Publication Data
Klingel, Cynthia Fitterer.
Halloween / by Cynthia Klingel and Robert B. Noyed.
    p. cm. — (Wonder books)
Includes bibliographical references and index.
ISBN 1-56766-955-7 (lib. bdg. : alk. paper)
1. Halloween—Juvenile literature. [1. Halloween. 2. Holidays.]
I. Noyed, Robert B. II. Title. III. Wonder books (Chanhassen, Minn.)
GT4965 .K55 2001
394.2646—dc21
                        00-011362